AF579415

Once upon a time there was a dino named Bobby,

and an angel named Victoria.

Bobby often crossed paths with Victoria,

but they never had the courage to speak to each other.

"Does Victoria not like me?" Thought Bobby.

"Does Bobby not like me?" Thought Victoria.

The next day Bobby was determined to make Victoria like him.

He would make funny faces.

He'd wave his hands to gain her attention.

But with every sign Bobby gave,

Victoria felt even more awkward.

"It's pointless", thought Bobby.

"I have to think of something else!"

He spent his day thinking how to approach Victoria.

And then an idea popped in his dino mind!

What Bobby had to do

was smile and talk to Victoria.

So the next day Bobby saw Victoria,

he gathered all of his courage...

...and said

"Hello Victoria!"

"Hello", said Victoria.

"Can we be friends?"
Asked Bobby.

"I'd love to!" answered Victoria with a big smile.

When they got back home,
both Bobby and Victoria
were happy.

"Bobby does like me!"
Thought Victoria.

"Victoria does like me!"
Thought Bobby.

And that is how, from two shy friends, Bobby and Victoria became

TWO BEST FRIENDS!

www.ingramcontent.com/pod-product-compliance
Lightning Source LLC
LaVergne TN
LVHW071111160826
845679LV00004B/1043
9798352523759